Jingle Bells

By Kathleen N. Daly
Illustrated by J. P. Miller
Based on the traditional Christmas carol

🌷 A GOLDEN BOOK • NEW YORK

Copyright © 1964, renewed 1992 by Random House LLC.
All rights reserved. Published in the United States by Golden Books, an imprint of Random House
Children's Books, a division of Random House LLC, 1745 Broadway, New York, NY 10019, and in Canada
by Random House of Canada Limited, Toronto, Penguin Random House Companies. Originally published
by Golden Press, Inc., New York, in 1964. Golden Books, A Golden Book, A Little Golden Book,
the G colophon, and the distinctive spine design are registered trademarks of Random House LLC.
A Little Golden Book Classic is a trademark of Random House LLC.
randomhousekids.com
Educators and librarians, for a variety of teaching tools, visit us at
RHTeachersLibrarians.com
Library of Congress Control Number: 2014946059
ISBN 978-0-553-51112-3 (trade) — ISBN 978-0-553-51113-0 (ebook)
Printed in the United States of America
10 9 8 7 6

Dashing through the snow comes the Bear family, **in a one-horse open sleigh.** There's Papa Bear and Mama Bear and two Baby Bears.

"O'er the fields we go!" shouts Papa Bear, cracking his whip. And the sleigh glides down over the snowy fields.

Laughing all the way, the Baby Bears sing
Christmas carols and nibble on cold plum pudding.

Hubert Horse loves to pull the sleigh. He flicks his
bob-tail merrily and the Baby Bears sing,

**"Bells on bob-tail ring,
Making spirits bright!"**
And dashing along they go.

Now they're in Rabbit Warren, a cozy little town, and the rabbits and their friends come out to say, "Hello!"

"Come aboard," says Papa Bear. "We're going for a ride." And Cuddly Bunny and three bunny sisters hop onto the sleigh.

Patrick Pig and his friend Katie Kitten hop in.
Then come Dennis Dog and Stewart Seal and
Richard Raccoon.

"**What fun it is to ride and sing a sleighing song tonight!**" says Esmeralda Ostrich, and she, too, hops aboard and starts singing.

She does not sing very well, but nobody minds because it is Christmas.

"Jingle bells, jingle bells, jingle all the way. Oh,
what fun it is to ride in a one-horse open sleigh!"
That's the sleighing song they sing.

O'er the fields they go, wrapped in their furs.
All of a sudden,
"Stop!" says a voice.
Who can it be?

It's a man with a white beard, in a red suit and big black boots, with a sack over his shoulder—it's Santa Claus!

"Help!" says Santa Claus. "I'm too tired to walk anymore!"

"What happened?" asks Papa Bear.

"My reindeer all caught cold, and their mother has put them to bed—"

"With bed socks and tea, I hope?" says Mama Bear.

"Yes," says Santa gloomily.

"Well, hop aboard! There's plenty of room,"
says Papa Bear.

And Santa hops aboard, sack and all.

Soon he is merrily singing the sleighing song:

**"Oh, what fun it is to ride
In a one-horse open sleigh!"**
And so for the first time Santa makes
all his visits in a one-horse open sleigh.
He brings Tommy a toy train, and
Dora gets a doll.

Rupert gets a rocking horse, and Bruce gets a boat.

When Santa's sack is empty, Santa and his helpers
climb into the sleigh, and Papa Bear cracks his whip,
and off they go, to take Santa home.

And when they get to Santa's house, what a lovely
surprise is waiting for them!
Mrs. Santa has cooked a Christmas dinner, with

lots of turkey and plum pudding and special fish for
Stewart Seal and Katie Kitten, and crunchy carrots
for the rabbits, and juicy corn for Patrick.

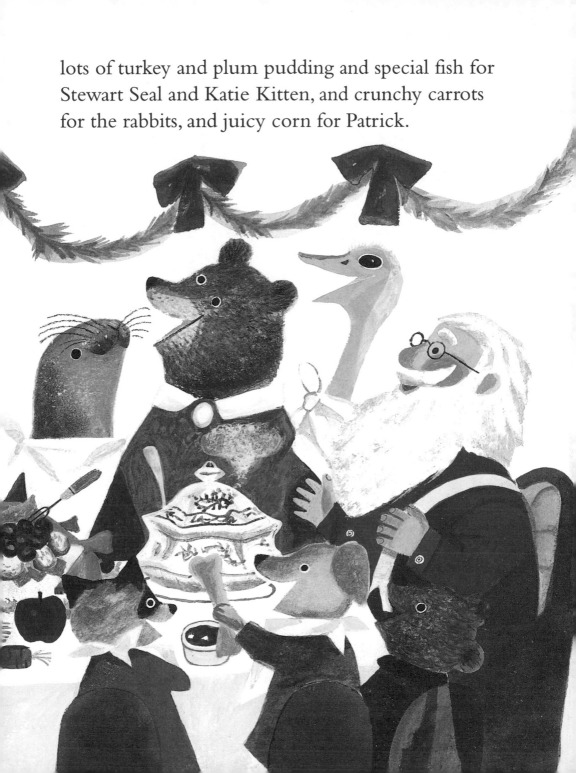

After dinner they gather around the biggest Christmas
tree you ever saw.

There are presents for all, and then there are balloons
to blow and games to play—my, what a party!

Before they leave, they peek in at the six little reindeer, all tucked up in bed and sniffling.

"Merry Christmas!" they call.

And the reindeer call, "Berry Christmas!"

Then they all pile into the sled—Papa Bear and
Mama Bear and two Baby Bears, Cuddly Bunny
and his three bunny sisters, Patrick Pig and Katie
Kitten, Dennis Dog and Stewart Seal and Richard
Raccoon, and Esmeralda Ostrich.

Papa Bear cracks his whip and off they go, in their one-horse open sleigh. And do you know the song they sing?

Jingle Bells